pseud Cleadas

Greedy of Gain

A sketch

pseud Cleadas

Greedy of Gain
A sketch

ISBN/EAN: 9783337097523

Printed in Europe, USA, Canada, Australia, Japan

Cover: Foto ©Andreas Hilbeck / pixelio.de

More available books at **www.hansebooks.com**

GREEDY OF GAIN:

A SKETCH.

BY

CLEADAS.

"He that is greedy of gain troubleth his own house; but he that
hateth gifts shall live."—PROVERBS.

LONDON:

BEVINGTON & CO., 5, JOHN STREET, ADELPHI, W.C.

1886.

GREEDY OF GAIN:

A SKETCH.

CHAPTER I.

A November evening is closing in with that dreary mist peculiar to the season, and is surrounding the thickly-wooded neighbourhood of Bramley, a picturesque village in the lovely and well known county of Blankshire.

Slowly wending his way, on a tired horse, in the direction of Bramley Hall, rides James West, thinking, as he proceeds, of that day's run with the Blankshire hounds. He has ridden with judgment and courage the good horse which knows him so well—for James West goes well over any country, but especially so in the neighbourhood of Bramley, where every inch of ground is familiar to

him, and has been since his earliest days,
when he used to come out on a Shetland
pony, and, attended by the family coachman,
ride the said pony with a liberality which
caused the coachman to prophecy great things
for the " young master " in the future.

Squire West, as he was usually called, was
now on the wrong side of thirty, and as fine a
specimen of an Englishman as one could wish
to see ; and, both his parents dying in his
early youth, had for the last fifteen years been
in every sense of the word his own master.
People wondered why he never married,
when, with an income such as his and a
country seat equal to any in the county, he
might so easily have made a " good match,"
as the phrase goes, and lived happily (or un-
happily) ever after.

Most of us, we might really say *all*, have,
however, experienced at least one knockdown
blow ere we have reached the age of thirty ;
and, whatever we may say on the subject,
there is no doubt that our whole afterlife is
to a great extent influenced by it. We may

laugh it off, smile at the whole subject, but the effect is there, and remains there in spite of any *ruses* of this sort.

James West had experienced his knock-down blow at the age of twenty-five, when he had that delightful experience of a London season and Lady Jane.

They were both the same age, but, as usually happens, the lady was so much the sharper of the two—the man throwing down his heart, his life, his all, so freely, nobly, and unhesitatingly, to have it trampled beneath an embroidered slipper, which trod none the less heavily because the wearer was the greatest beauty in London, and the one shrine before which he worshipped.

It was a terrible strain—a strain such as tests to the uttermost the stuff a man is made of, and James West stood it well, and outwardly, at anyrate, made no sign of the agony that raged within. But James West came of a race who scorned to show how much they suffered; whatever it was, it was borne in secret. Had not Henry West, in years gone

by, endured all the agony of the rack
sooner than betray a state secret?—and died
under the torture, merely remarking that
"thus had Englishmen ever died in defence
of aught they considered sacred;" and now,
in this nineteenth century of ours, surely
James West, the descendant of such a line,
was not going to exhibit how deeply he felt
the wisdom of a woman—deserting four thousand a year and youth for fifty thousand a
year and age. It is simply the way of the
world, too, every story is good until another
is told, and James West, with a fair income
and a rather nice place in the country, faded
into insignificance before Mr. Bullion with
unlimited means, carriages by the score, and
footmen by the dozen; and nobody was so
weak as to take the love and devotion of a
life into the account—nobody ever is.

And what had been the effect upon James
West? Outwardly very little; he was a trifle
quieter than before when he returned from
that year's mysterious absence, no one knew
where, which every civilised man now takes

when a social earthquake happens, and which appears to right everything, from an eloping wife to a breaking bank,—the former, of course, being the much greater miracle of the two.

How the lady fared we do not trouble to inquire. She had all the money she could wish to outshine the immediate circle of her bosom friends, and so we may take it that she was as happy as she deserved to be at any rate. As for Mr. Bullion, I suppose he was content. He liked everything of the best; his house, horses, and yacht had all been perfect, and now his wife was quite *en suite*.

Whether there was a

> " Little rift within the lute,
>   That, wid'ning, made the music mute,"

or whether there had ever been any music at all before the period of the rift, are questions that we cannot well enter upon. He may have loved, but he was a stout man, " turned of sixty," who snored after dinner, and I am not certain whether such creatures can love, so we will leave it an open question.

What an altered place Bramley Hall seemed to James West when he returned from that year's absence! For he was one of those silent natures that feel all the more deeply for their outward impassiveness, and *she* had been at Bramley in those halcyon days of his early love. Now each object was but a milestone on the dreary road, leading back to that ever to be remembered past which his steps would retrace no more.

But, whatever his private feeling might be, there were local duties to be performed, and these he did as of yore ; and everyone hoped he had " had a good time," and he said he had enjoyed himself amazingly. So everything settled down into its old track, and that was now eight years ago. Eight years is a long time as things go, and James West left his horse at the stables, and went up the fine old staircase to dress for dinner, thinking that there were other things in life worth living for than a woman's smile.

If we could only induce our younger friends to believe this! Some such thoughts passed through my mind last night at the club, when I saw young Audrey, aged twenty-two, rushing about the building, in dress clothes, at 4.30 p.m., and all because he was to be allowed the extreme felicity of taking Miss Vavasour (aged, in charity, thirty-seven) to the theatre, to see that piece ever in season, and much more of a tragedy than most people imagine, entitled " Cupid Reigns; " and I could not help feeling a sort of pity for the poor boy as I thought of all that was in store for him, before that great revolution, which most of us experience sooner or later, when Cupid is deposed, never to reign again !

CHAPTER II.

EVERYONE said that Bullion Castle—re-named immediately after taking possession by Mr. Bullion—was one of the finest and most magnificent palaces in the hands of any commoner.

Standing on an eminence, from which the surrounding country lay like a map before the spectator, the walls covered with ivy and creepers; the stained glass windows (in which the crest of Bullion, a boar's head with a lemon in its mouth, had replaced the stately armorial insignia of an old but now exiled race), everything in fact was charming; and if there was a little too much gilding and splendour generally internally, it was more than counterbalanced in the eyes of guests by the age of the wines and the ability of the cook.

Mr. Bullion was still connected with the City, and went thither several times a week, leaving Lady Jane to herself, as, indeed, she was left at all times. But there was plenty of society, and the fact of Mr. Bullion having married a lady made an excellent excuse for the county to be on very friendly terms with the Castle.

In one respect Mr. Bullion was a model husband. He never wanted to know what she was doing or intended doing, and beyond an occasional questioning of his valet, whilst he dressed for dinner on his return from London, as to the probable number of visitors to dine that night, interested himself very little in the management of affairs.

To-night there has been a dinner party, and everyone has come into the drawing-room to listen with as much pleasure as we generally do to amateur music, which as we know is always delightful and pleases everyone, especially when it is finished.

Mr. Bullion has dexterously concealed himself in a curtained recess, and, save for an occasional smothered snore, might as well have been concealed in another sort of recess in Mother Earth, which is not usually curtained, and is invariably, I believe, much colder.

Lady Jane well, but not *too well* dressed— for she is a lady, remember—after having persuaded a young lady to charm the company with the piano, is gracefully resting on a sofa, talking easily and well to Major Sir Harry Vale, who has driven over from the neighbouring garrison town of Waterfield to be present.

A man on whom one would look with interest is Sir Harry. His age might be anything from thirty-six to forty. His face and features clearly cut, such as we all agree to call a " high type " of countenance, and which comes from generations of " blue blood " unsullied by intermixture with the " hewers of wood and drawers of water."

He is watching her with evident admiration,

as any man not an idiot would have done,
for Lady Jane is a lovely woman—the beauty
of eight years ago is only developed now
and more pronounced.

"Then you will come to our steeplechases?"
he is saying, a trifle perhaps more anxiously
than such a simple question calls for; "if it
is only to see my fight for victory."

And Lady Jane, raising those beautiful
eyes, deepened with an expression which is
almost reproach, answers: "Yes, if you wish
it, I will come," and the remark is accentuated
by a peaceful snore from the direction of the
curtained recess where Mr. Bullion is re-
posing.

The hour has come for departure, that
happy hour, if you are a bachelor, when,
having been assisted into a coat—probably
someone else's—you can put your feet up in
the brougham and enjoy that cigar you have
been longing for all the evening. There is a
white frost; the road rings under the feet of
the good horse that is doing his twelve miles
an hour so easily, and you meditate how

emblematic the recent entertainment and
your cigar are of the world's vanities, which
all invariably end in smoke !

Alas ! for the Major ! Unfortunately for
him, no such thoughts crossed his mind as
he drove back that lovely night to his
quarters in Waterfield. He is beginning to
feel the influence of those eyes that, eight
years ago, wrought such havoc with James
West. He is beginning, and at a fatal age,
too, to dream that dream which we all have
dreamed in our turn, since Adam, in all the
pristine innocence of his heart, took that fatal
nap in the midst of his gardening operations.

Sir Harry felt annoyed, very much annoyed,
and the more so because he could not clearly
define the person who was to blame for this
annoyance. Was it himself, or Lady Jane, or
poor, harmless Mr. Bullion, who at that
precise moment was again peacefully snoring,
this time under the connubial counterpane ;
whilst James West, three counties off, was
deep in the mysteries of "stirrup leathers,"
and "plain flap saddles," with his old butler,

who had been with the Wests for fifty years,
and was, as he himself expressed it, " something of a sportsman."

Deep in this subject; deep in any subject
which prevented thoughts of the past—for he
was not cured yet, and even now thoughts
went back to the past—sometimes,—when the
sun was setting in a crimson splendour that
tinged the mullioned windows of Bramley
like blood ; back to all those blissful moments
which would come again no more—no more !

Sir Harry was a man of action, and took a
decision very quickly, and as he drove into
the barrack square that night he had decided
what course he should pursue in the future,
and, having made up his mind, went slowly
up to his quarters and slept the sleep of the
righteous in peace.

And what of Lady Jane ? Her ladyship
did not have a good night on that occasion ;
the rooms had perhaps been too hot, or
possibly the snoring of the good Mr. Bullion
was loud enough to banish rest, I cannot say ;
but, be this as it may, the fact remains that

she was uneasy and restless, waking with a
start from troubled dreams and terrifying
visions. It was most unfair that this should
be so. A lady whose repute was as good,
and whose morals were as sound as Lady
Jane's, was surely entitled to a quiet night's
rest, after doing her duty all the evening, and
dispensing hospitality freely, without grudging
or of necessity! However, be the cause what
it might of her night's restlessness, she was
entirely recovered in the morning, when she
took her customary cheque from Mr. Bullion,
with the usual matter-of-course manner, as
though everyone was allowed £200 a month for
mere dress expenses. Lady Jane, although she
came of a good stock, had nothing of her
own, and Mr. Bullion had agreed, upon her
marriage, to allow her two hundred a month
for pin-money. Mr. Bullion, on those days
that he was not in London, used to wander
about his park and home-farm, in a somewhat
lonely and disconsolate manner, feeling, in a
vague kind of way, that his wife was perhaps
not so devoted to him as she might have been

to James West, had that match ever come off. For he was well aware that he had taken West's bride, and, being an honest man, often regretted the fact, and felt a genuine pity for the poor young fellow, as he would have put it. Often, too, did he regret that his marriage had been childless, and that his vast wealth must eventually go to a stranger. But he was a man who had sufficient intellect not to endeavour to fight the inevitable, and ended his cogitations by turning towards the house and hoping that West had recovered by this time.

CHAPTER III.

In a small but picturesque cottage on the Bullion estate dwelt Richard Reef, who as a lad had swept out the then small office which was all that in those days represented the now palatial offices of Bullion & Co.

He had in time become messenger to the house, and, at the age of seventy, Mr. Bullion, who was a good master, pensioned him and gave him the small cottage before-mentioned, in which he might end his days in peace.

Hardly more than once in his busy life had Reef seen the country, and great was his glee when, accompanied by his only daughter Rosa, he took up his abode at the cottage.

His wife had died many years before, and his sole care and pride was now his daughter, and a better girl could no man wish for as a nurse to ease the last few years of life.

But at present Richard Reef had no intention of dying : far from it, he was full of plans for the next summer—the woods they would visit together, the sketches she should make, and the altogether blissful time they would have in company.

A pretty cottage was his abode—" Rose Cottage" by name—" Rosa " he said it should have been, not above a quarter of a mile from the castle.

Such a cottage as poets and painters are always describing, with creepers winding round the entrance and stealing far away up the roof; but inside especially charming— charming with that peculiar grace which a pretty girl always contrives to throw over any spot she inhabits.

A cottage with odd nooks and corners, with brackets on the walls, and delicate, inexpensive curtains, shading the little diamond-paned windows.

Often of an evening, for that hour that

hangs always somewhat heavily in the country, before it is time to dress for dinner, would Mr. Bullion stroll over the park to visit Richard Reef, and, sitting in the small parlour, talking over early days with his old servant, till the dressing-bell, pealing over hill and dale, would summon him homewards to all the splendours of dinner *à la Russe*.

* * * * *

What a pretty picture Rosa makes to-night, sitting at the tea-table in her simple white gown, whilst Reef, lost in admiration, gazes at her with all the deep, strong affection of a parent, and thinks pleasantly to himself what a pretty woman she will make a few years hence; for, though she appears older, she is in reality little more than sixteen.

"Dear father," says she, as the old man, having finished his tea, is preparing to smoke a pipe, "how happy we are. I wonder whether the people at the Castle have half the pleasure, amid all their splendour, that we have in this quiet nook."

And so the conversation drifts away into

speculations of various matters, until, nine o'clock having struck, the girl affectionately kisses Reef and retires for the night.

Left to himself, Richard Reef lights a fresh pipe and slowly thinks over the past.

No one looking at the fine open face of Richard Reef, would suspect him of having a secret; but so it is. Not a very dreadful secret, truly, but one that weighs on his mind and troubles him as time goes on, and he doubts more and more whether he is justified in keeping it longer to himself.

His mind goes back to that winter night, now sixteen years ago, when he found that little infant neglected, in a bundle at his door; of the consultations with his wife; of their own childless condition; how he had suggested that the child had been almost given to them by Providence; and how they had finally decided to adopt it as their own, and had done so; and how, at the age of sixteen, the girl had no idea but that she was the child of Richard, and mourned for his wife as for her mother.

Richard Reef and his wife were in their way
discerning people, and noticed the quality of
the garb in which the infant was dressed, and
guessed rightly that it was somewhat superior
to the common kind; but never had a clue of
any sort been found, and the slight scar, now
almost obliterated by time on the child's forehead, which they had both looked upon as
the mark by which some day identification
would be made, had led to nothing. What
should Reef do? This was the question per-
petually in his mind. He was growing old;
the end might come at any time, and should
he go to his grave, leaving the child in igno-
rance of her doubtful parentage? This now
recurred with more and more force to his
mind, and still he could find no satisfactory
conclusion to the question.

Was it selfishness or love at the root of the
matter? Was he afraid that she might somehow change towards him when she discovered
the truth? It may have been; but if it
were, he wronged the girl, whose kindly
nature would have loved him all the more

for his kindness to her in her helpless
state.

We are all apt to be troubled by a question
which for the life of us we cannot solve alone,
and which perhaps we are too proud to seek
advice upon. But Reef was not too proud to
seek advice; he did not like to trouble Mr.
Bullion with his affairs, and moreover hated
the idea of letting any one else into the secret
he had held so long.

He had done his duty towards his adopted
child; he had educated her very fairly, not
without, I believe, a mysterious belief that
some day a carriage with gorgeous footmen,
and prancing bays, would come mysteriously
from nowhere in particular, and claim his
child as the princess of some mighty inheri-
tance. But up to the present no such event
had occurred, and on this particular night,
Richard Reef went to bed with his mind as
undecided as usual on the great question.

CHAPTER IV.

THE morning sun is streaming into the breakfast room at Bramley Hall, lighting up the
ancient pictures and ingenious wood carvings
on the walls. At the table sits James West,
alone. He has finished breakfast, and is just
going through, for the second time, the pile
of letters which that morning's post has
brought him. One especially chains his attention, and so deeply is he engaged in its
perusal, that his spaniel on the rug by the
fire is strongly tempted to make a depredation
on the remains of the breakfast, and stands
with one eye on the table and the other on
his master, with an expression that says
plainly, "If I only dare!" But he thinks
better of it, and lies down again, with a dis-

contented grunt, which, by the way, fails to produce any effect whatever.

The letter which claims so much attention from West is very short and simple. It is dated from West Wick House, West Wick, near Waterfield, and runs as follows :—

"MY DEAR WEST,

"They are all bothering me to write and ask you to come to us for the steeplechases, on the 24th. I know what a stay-at-home fellow you are, but you might for once in a way do us the pleasure of breaking your rule. Two of my horses are going to run, and besides I have a horse I wish to get rid of, as I have one above my number, and I think you would like him. Write and say you will come for a couple of days at any rate.

"Very faithfully yours,

"ALFRED WRIGHT.

"P.S.—The girls have agreed never to speak to you again if you don't come.

"A. W."

Surely he was himself again by this time, and could see Lady Jane, at any rate in the distance, without experiencing any very alarming symptoms. Why should he shut himself up for ever? Some such thoughts as these were in West's mind, as he read this letter, for he was a thorough sportsman, and loved a steeplechase, or a race of any kind, very much. So he made up his mind to say, "Yes," and brave the smiles and wiles of his cousin's five daughters, and wrote that morning, accepting the invitation.

It was quite dark when West drove up the avenue at West Wick House, the night before the steeplechases, and after a hearty welcome from his relative, he went off to dress for dinner. They were only a family party that night, and he had to stand all the concentrated chaff of the five Miss Wrights, who were good at everything, from riding across country, well in front, to tennis and dancing, but especially good at chaff. And the ties of relationship having removed all scruples, he had, what he himself would have described as, a very warm time of it.

"His dress coat is really within two years of the fashion," exclaimed Miss Eveline, gazing critically at his costume in the drawing-room, on his descent thither before dinner.

"And he actually wears Court shoes!" cried, Nelly, the youngest daughter. Why, James, we all fancied that during your retirement, at your ancient Hall, you had discarded the usages of civilization, and returned to the artistic customs of the early Britons."

"Far from it," said West, really amused; "the modern lady seems to me to be nearer the era of painted skins."

"We will have none of your cynicism here," replies the girl, "and as to 'the modern lady,' as you call her; I don't believe you have seen one these eight years, so your opinion is quite worthless. But as pure simplicity seems to be all your fancy, before you go home we will show you something quite too charming—by name, Rosa Reef. No, she's not 'one of us,' as you call it; but you will

find her none the less captivating on that
account, and her father is a charming old
man."

A further description of Rosa was here in-
terrupted by the announcement of dinner,
and with one of his fair relatives on each
arm, West was conducted to the dining room.
They were good girls, these Wrights, and
they felt for the man, about whose unfortunate
affair they had heard all particulars from their
mother, and thinking that he must be terribly
in want of fun and amusement, determined
that during his stay with them he should at
anyrate have nothing to complain of on this
score.

That night, in the smoking-room, when the
two cousins were alone together, and the
light blue smoke from their cigars wreath-
ing upwards towards the moulded ceiling,
the host suddenly turned upon the guest, and
asked quickly: "West, old fellow, have you
quite got over that miserable affair of eight
years ago? And West, thoroughly believing
he is speaking the truth, answers: "Upon

my word I have, Alfred; but why do you ask?" "Because you may see her at the races to-morrow, and I feared if you had still a lingering memory, it might be painful." Ye gods, a lingering memory! Oh, Mr. Wright, you are an excellent man, a just man; you understand the rotation of crops, the management of the local Bench, and you can make a fairly intelligible speech at the agricultural dinner; but you are not romantic, you cannot say you are, even if we appeal directly to yourself. To think a man of West's temperament could have such an utterly crushing blow as his, and then recover, and recover so well that no " lingering memory " remains!

West might think himself recovered—but as to a lingering memory! Whilst life remains; whilst the scent drifts seductively across from the beanfield at sunset; whilst the white rose perfume fills the opera box; whilst the senses remain, so long will the "lingering memory" last—last till the darkening room, and hushed voices of friends, tell us that the end is near, that we shall never ride

at Ripley brook again, and never pound the
field at that hogbacked stile in the Westrop
road; that for us the shades that are falling
so fast and thick are the shades of an eternal
night, then, and not till then, will the "lingering memory" drift from us, and become merged
in the becalmed ocean of eternity.

"I never could understand that infatuation,"
said Mr. Wright, reflectively, thinking that
now it was over it was safe ground to tread;
" and then, West, you know the story about
her when she was quite a girl. You always
disbelieved the scandal; but those Egremonts
are a fast lot, and you forget how influence
and absence from England can hush up anything."

I don't know whether West's thoughts
were taken up just then with a "lingering
memory," but his answers were abstracted and
far from the point; so after a short time his
host suggested bed, and West agreeing with
alacrity, was soon tossing in an uneasy
slumber that ended before the dawn.

They were a cheerful party at the breakfast

on the morning of the steeplechases; the Misses Wright in most becoming gowns, specially made for the occasion.

A pretty place was Westwick House; white, with ivy creeping gracefully over the greater part of it. Especially a house to be at home in; with large comfortable rooms, and a particularly well-stocked library; with easy lounges, where you could doze over your book, whilst the heavy curtains kept out the glare of the sun, and tempered the heat in summer, or repelled the whistling winds in winter, when, assembled round the fire, the fair daughters of the house would recount ghost stories sufficient to make your hair stand on end (if you had any). Indeed, Mr. Wright was wont to say that his own baldness was chiefly attributable to the thrilling stories he had listened to in this room.

CHAPTER V.

IT is past midnight at Bullion Castle, the night before the steeplechases, and in a lovely boudoir, where the mellow light comes through ruby coloured glass shades, sits Lady Jane, amid solid magnificence. She is alone, having dismissed her maid, and is half undressed, and musing.

Amid such splendour, how happy those musings should be! How contented should she feel! But, strangely enough, Lady Jane is not at all happy or contented to-night. She is thinking deeply, and thinking of very unpleasant things—thinking of the past.

Wondering what that strange feeling is which has come upon her lately with regard to Sir Harry Vale. Wondering why he is in

her thoughts now, at this hour, when everyone else is sleeping peaceably. Why she is
musing over the words he said, last night, and
of the lingering smile, that was almost a caress,
when they parted. Thinking of many departed love affairs, and of James West—how
devotedly he had loved her, and how she had
thrown him over for the City millionaire.
Thinking of a period even earlier than the
era of James West, when she had really
loved, loved deeply, for the first time; loved
with all the ardour of a schoolgirl—and how
suddenly she had awoke from that dream,
and what an unpleasant and realistic waking
it was! Of that period of seclusion which was
absolutely necessary to repair her broken
heart, etc., etc. Well, Lady Jane never
thinks of that period now, and she is wise to
banish that memory, which is anything but
pleasant. Having come to this conclusion,
she gracefully seeks her couch, and passes the
night in unhappy dreams and distressed and
feverish slumbers.

What a contrast, such a life as Lady Jane's

is to any of the humble lives surrounding
her—compared, let us say, with that of Rosa
Reef—of poor, humble, contented little Rosa,
who outshines no one except by such beauty
as nature gave her; whose jewels comprise
only a small simple ruby and diamond ring,
such as a girl might wear, and which had
been found fastened round her neck when
Reef first discovered her, and had been
rigorously preserved by him ever since, and
which she values more, far more than Lady
Jane does her magnificent diamonds which
Mr. Bullion gave her, with no sparing hand,
in the early days of their marriage.

Notwithstanding all that has been said,
Lady Jane is not entirely a woman of the
world, worldly; her nature is, to a certain
extent, kindly, more especially when any spice
of patronage can mingle with her kindness,
and she has been very kind indeed to Rosa
Reef, and nothing has pleased Mr. Bullion
more in his wife's conduct, than the stories he
hears whenever he calls at Rosa's cottage, of
her goodness to Reef's daughter. How she

has had her to the Castle, to see the wonderful things in the drawing-rooms, or the old masters in the picture gallery. How she has commissioned her to paint several little pictures from various points in the park and neighbourhood; and how now she is actually contemplating having her taught music, and presenting her with a piano. Old Reef thinks to himself, after Rosa has retired of a night, and he is smoking that last pipe before retiring himself, how remarkably lucky it is that Lady Jane should have taken such a fancy to the girl, and how, as he puts it, "when her ladyship has done with her, she will be fit to marry any one in the land."

It would be safe to take long odds that there are no happier people in the world than Reef and Rosa, whose lives are one blissful round of entertainment all the year.

For you and I know, none better, that happiness does not come from fine estates, princely retinues, and gorgeous equipages; these things appear the only thing necessary to Vavasour, of the Home Office, who struggles on £150 a

year, or to Jones, the young man from the
drapery establishment round the corner, who
exists on something less; but those who can
reason, those who have a mind, to say nothing
of those who have experienced—to these it is
clear that such things can only protect from
one of all those evils that flesh is heir to—
poverty!

I don't think Richard Reef was a sufficiently
deep thinker to come to any such conclusion
as this; but without it he was contented, and
if he did want anything—we all want something—it was that some impossible nobleman
should come from some impossible place, and
straightway bear off Rosa as his bride, before
the gathering clouds of age should close
around him in an eternal night.

Ah, Reef, you may well be proud of the
child of your adoption; and you are quite
right when you say she looks a lady, every
inch of her. The white forehead, with the
dark hair in wavy tresses; those wonderful
eyes, and that graceful manner. I don't at
all wonder that Smith, the young farmer from

Beachly farm, should be over head and ears in a hopeless, unrequited passion. Hopeless, because he has never, in spite of desperate endeavours, been able to get even on speaking terms with his enslaver. A hopeless, soul-blighting passion; a passion such as causes him to be regular in his attendance at the parish church, because for two hours during service he can have an uninterrupted view of Rosa, who is totally unaware of the effect she has produced; a passion that causes him to neglect the " ordinary," at the " Crown," in Waterfield, on market days, and prefer long walks to nowhere in particular; a passion that causes his respectable and elderly house-keeper to opine, in private, that things are not going well with Arthur, and fear, still more privately, that he was " taking to drink." " Taking to drink ! " I should think he was. Drinking deep draughts of that eternal spring, whose effects are as various as the hues of the rainbow, and, generally, not half so pretty; a passion such as causes him to wander in a purposeless manner in the im-

mediate vicinity of Rose cottage, at night,
and thereby arouse the suspicions of the
local representative of the law.

But nothing comes of it; it goes off harm-
lessly in the end, and he eventually consoles
himself with Dolly Brightwell from the "Golden
Lion," just as if nothing had occurred.

Rosa has the run of the pleasure gardens
at the Castle, but seldom avails herself of the
privilege, preferring to wander only in the
now usually deserted rosary, an enclosed
garden, in close vicinity to the Castle. About
the narrow walks she loves to roam, and muse
on all the bye-gone glories of the Castle. Of
all the titled worthies who had strolled in
that very rosary, of their past hopes and
fears—hopes and fears that had long since
gone to nothingness and decay.

To muse on the great works of Tennyson—
of Guinevere, the guilty; of Arthur amongst
his barons; of Arthur going forth, broken-
hearted as he was, to fight that "last great
battle in the west," whence he never more
returned.

And, musing, thus, she gradually formed her mind to a higher standard than that reached by most young ladies who have had an extensive (and **expensive**) education, and who are " finished " in a manner highly satisfactory to **their** governesses, if to no one else.

CHAPTER VI.

It was a charming day, and Waterfield was arrayed in its most becoming costumes in honour of the steeplechases.

What a scene of animation presented itself to the occupants of the Westwick House waggonette, as they drove on to the course, in close proximity to the Grand Stand !

It was half an hour yet to the first race ; but every one appeared to have something to do—a motley assembly, truly !

Here a nigger in a heterogeneous costume, and with a large banjo, endeavouring to attract the attention of the occupants of the carriages by comic songs of a more or less disagreeable character. There, a gipsy woman, trying to persuade the " pretty gentleman " to have his fortune told, and the " pretty gentleman " (who by the way is as ugly as sin, with one eye immovable in his head), quite overcome by the unaccustomed flattery, is endeavouring to find a half-crown from the recesses of his overcoat.

Great was the surprise of everyone on the course, when the Bullion drag (driven by the Bullion coachman) appeared on the course, to notice Mr. Bullion seated amid the smart people on the roof.

Never before had Mr. Bullion attended a local race meeting ; but the surprise of the public was nothing compared to the surprise which had been caused at the Castle that morning at breakfast, when Mr. Bullion had come down and announced his intention of being present.

Why it was, no one could imagine ; but of course everyone appeared delighted at the idea, and Mr. Bullion went.

It is difficult to say why he went. It may be that he had come gradually to realize that it was hardly wise on his part to leave his wife so entirely to her own friends and her own amusements ; it may be that even he had noticed the growing friendship between Sir Harry Vale and herself.

Whatever the reason, there was Mr. Bullion, looking extremely happy and slightly surprised at himself, standing on the top of his drag, talking to Sir Harry.

The first race is just coming on, and cries of, " two to one bar one," resound on all sides.

Only five runners in this race ; there they go, and from our position how slow the pace appears to be, and what very little courage seems required to ride over such small fences as they look from here ! And yet we are aware that the brook they have just cleared in a line is a good sixteen feet wide, and the fence in the corner that they are approaching so rapidly, is so big that, when we looked at it yesterday, we mentally congratulated our-selves that our day is past, and that we have won our laurels, whatever they may be worth, long since, and are still whole in body.

It is most exciting, and Mr. Bullion feels it

so, and even expresses a wish to " have something on the next race," a wish in which Sir
Harry immediately accommodates him *on the
spot*, " to save the trouble of going into the
ring, don't you know," and accommodates
him so effectually that Mr. Bullion at once
realises the dangers of a love of speculation
in this direction.

Poor James West! It is not an entirely
happy day for him. He has never seen Lady
Jane before since the great event in their
lives, and now he only sees her at a distance;
but it is sufficient to make him feel very un-
comfortable. But he is a thorough sportsman, and the racing makes up to him in a
great measure for anything, and the Misses
Wright keep up a constant running fire of
badinage, which prevents him dwelling entirely upon the past. .

None the less, he is remarkably pleased
when at 4·30, having seen most of the fun,
they leave the course and return to Westwick
House.

" Mr. West, you must promise to keep your

heart," says Eveline, the afternoon after the races, as she and one of her sisters are walking with him in the direction of Rose Cottage.

"I think I can be trusted," he replies, gaily; "I am not particularly likely to rob you of your charming piece of simplicity in muslin, either by cajolery or force of arms. You may keep her for ever so far as I am concerned."

They were brave words; but he made one great mistake, a mistake which we are all apt to make; he fancied he was entirely master of himself.

What a pretty girl Rosa looked that afternoon, when they reached the cottage! And how prettily she asked them to have some tea, and how willingly they consented! And what a cheerful party it was; old Reef in the highest of high spirits, at observing what a good impression Rosa was making.

West is abstracted and rather quiet; his thoughts going back, for some mysterious reason, to the past; struggling with some strange association of a byegone day, which he cannot clearly call to mind.

Tea in a cottage! What can be pleasanter. Especially when the maker of the tea is one of the prettiest girls in the county. What to us is ambition at such a moment? What is it to us at such a moment that her grace, the Countess of Cablemore, omitted us from that dinner party to meet Royalty, last week; or that a new candidate is in the field for Bryants, the borough that has returned us so undisputedly these twenty years; that Emily was decidedly cold to us last night? These things rank as nothing to us now. Is not the tea sweeter than the tenderness, as the peaches are preferable to the politics, and as for the Countess of Cablemore—she is nowhere compared to the cakes.

To say that West was surprised would be a very mild way of expressing his sentiments at the appearance and manners of Rosa Reef; but on the return to Westwick House, he said very little on the subject, though, like the owl in the story, he doubtless thought the more.

Very pleased **was** West with his visit to the Wrights, and it was much to the astonishment of them all when, on his departure for Bramley, he announced his intention **of very** soon coming to **see** them again.

"**We** thought the **cup was** broken, we thought the tale was told ;
But the new wine—the new wine—it tasteth **like** the old."

This was the rhyme that "beat **time** to nothing in his head," all the way back to Bramley.

CHAPTER VII.

IT is 9·30, and a lovely night, six months later than the date of the Waterfield steeple-chases, 9·30 of a lovely moonlight night in May. There is that hush over everything which is always noticeable on a fine evening in the country. There has been a dinner party at the Castle; a gorgeous dinner party, at which each woman present wore every jewel she possessed, and only wished the number had been double.

Now they have broken into groups; some listening to more (or less) enchanting music in the drawing-rooms; others preferring the cooler atmosphere of the terrace overlooking the rose garden.

Mr. Bullion is dozing quietly and unnoticed

in a distant corner of one of the drawing-rooms. Rosa, oppressed by the day's heat, has strolled—an unusual thing at this hour —to her favourite spot, the rose garden, to enjoy the drowsy perfume of the roses.

What a picture she would have made, seated on a rustic seat, just below the terrace, almost dozing, but not quite; happy, at peace with all the world.

Suddenly she is wide awake, and can hardly prevent a cry escaping her. What is it that causes such a change to overspread her features? Only a half-whispered conversation going on, just above her head, on the terrace, and the speakers are Lady Jane and Sir Harry Vale.

Silently as the night she glides unseen from the spot, and retraces her steps to the cottage where Reef is even now anxiously watching for her.

The last words are ringing still in her ears, ringing in her ears as no other words had ever rung before, and they were only these—" On Wednesday week, then; be it so "—and they were the words of Lady Jane.

A whirl of conflicting thoughts confused and agitated Rosa. This woman was almost her friend; she had shown her all the kindness in her power; what was the path that duty pointed out ? *She* could not warn poor Mr. Bullion of the wrong and ridicule that was to be brought upon him. There was only one thing to be done; she must confess the whole conversation she had overheard to old Reef.

Greatly did she dread the task; but it had to be done, and she alone could do it.

That night Rosa and Reef sat together in deep consultation until the morning sun broke through the diamond panes of their little window.

And what of Lady Jane? Oh, Lady Jane, think again ere it be too late ! Think, before you leave for ever the good old man who has humoured every wish and denied you nothing !

But the fatal taint is in the blood, and with

D

the ease with which she abandoned West, without a tear, without a sigh, will she now within eight days leave her husband. Leave him for the *roué* with the *distingué* face, for the man who in a month will tire of her, as he has tired of others as beautiful; tire, to fling her aside, like an old glove, or the end of a cigar.

It is with great surprise on the following day to the dinner-party, that Mr. Bullion, sitting alone in the afternoon, in the Castle library—for Lady Jane is away at a garden-party, six miles off—hears that Richard Reef wishes for a private interview, and most anxious to hear the purport of it, desires him to be shown up at once. Deeply impressed as Reef is at the nature of his communication to Mr. Bullion, he is still more impressed by the splendour of the room into which he is shown, and for some time he is unable to articulate anything. Then at last he begins— begins as softly as he can—and gradually leads up to what Rosa had heard arranged the night before—the flight of that day week.

Mr. Bullion listened quietly—as quietly as

he would have done to the disclosure of a plot of one of his clerks to disappear with the ready cash of his business establishment.

"Is that all you can tell me?" he says, when Reef has done.

"That is all, sir" answers Reef, aghast at his composure.

"I will see my solicitor," mutters Mr. Bullion, more to himself than Reef; "I have not been feeling quite myself lately," continues Mr. Bullion, this time addressing himself to his old servant; "but I shall be better soon—better soon," he repeats, somewhat vaguely, putting his hand to his forehead, and Reef thinks he had better go. Mr. Bullion, for the first time since Reef had known him, rises rapidly and grasps his hand, and he sees that there is something almost like a tear in his eye as he does so. "Good-bye, Reef, good-bye, we shall meet again ere long," and with these words they part, and Reef goes home in the most unhappy frame of mind he has been in since occupying Rose Cottage.

By no sign did Mr. Bullion show his wife

that he was aware of the lasting insult she was about to cast upon his name; and as for Mr. Moorcraft, head of the highly respectable firm of solicitors, Moorcraft & Rye, why, he had been down constantly, and his presence for a day at this juncture appeared no more than an ordinary visit to Lady Jane.

West is again at Westwick House; quite himself again now, more cheerful than he has been these last eight years, his only peculiarity being an almost daily absence of an hour or two, passed by him in walking in the woods, and admiring the beauties of nature, and I use the term in its widest sense.

And Rosa—dear, dainty, captivating little Rosa—she is beginning to learn by slow and mysterious degrees that there may be an affection even more entirely engrossing than that which she feels for Richard Reef, and of an entirely different kind, and she is rather distressed, very much surprised, and not a little frightened by this discovery.

And Richard Reef—puzzling his brains nightly with regard to the doubtful question

of the child's paternity, and wondering in a
vague way whether it will be ever discovered,
or go down to the grave with him a secret.
Ah, Reef! why don't you let the child gratify
her vanity, and wear that one only ruby and
diamond ring that she possesses?

CHAPTER VIII.

LADY JANE is about to dupe Mr. Bullion as she did James West. Dupe him in a different way certainly, but none the less effectually.

Her life had been one long deception, and when at times she was unwell, or, as she herself described it " not quite up to concert pitch," she was liable to very unpleasant memories, was Lady Jane.

She was constantly wondering since the engagement was broken off, eight years ago, whether West had by any side wind heard a very unpleasant piece of scandal about her, which had had rather too great a currency to be pleasant, some years before she had met him, a scandal which was all the more unpleasant because it was true.

A nasty, haunting scandal it was, too, which was always even now upon her mind.

For there had been a mysterious disappearance of one of the chief, indeed *the* chief person connected with the event, which troubled her now, as it had ever since.

And Lady Jane would have given her best jewel, aye and gladly, too, to know *for certain* on one point.

And here was Lady Jane worrying herself for years about a matter which, had she but known, would have instantly been solved by the simple expedient of walking across her rose garden to the humble abode of Richard Reef!

What a lovely night it is; a lovely night down at Bramley, with the moon shining on the fretwork of the windows at the Hall; shining with reflected glory on the waters of the lake; shining on the stone terrace along the south front, where James West and a couple of neighbours are smoking their cigars and drinking their coffee after a hardly contested tennis match. A lovely night at

Bullion Castle; the moon's rays making the trees look ghostly in her beams. Even a lovely night at Victoria Station; a night so hot that the porters have long since discarded their jackets, and the passengers by the Dover train are congratulating themselves and each other on the "remarkably easy passage across they will have." But two passengers, a lady of handsome appearance, and a gentleman with a *distingué* face, who are in a "retained" compartment, have decided not to cross that night, but to stay at the "Lord Warden" at Dover. The train speeds on, and, hardened though she is, Lady Jane cannot help thinking of the Castle and Mr. Bullion. He has returned from London long ago, she is thinking; long ago he must have discovered the insult and disgrace she has brought upon his name. How has he taken it? This is the question which constantly recurs to her mind. It is past the usual dinner hour. What is he doing? He cannot, surely, be taking his customary nap, as though nothing had occurred. Ah, Lady

Jane! go to the arms of your lover; think no more of your lawful husband; forget the vows you made at the altar. Go to your lover! Think no more of any one inside the pale of civilised society; you have nothing in common; henceforth you are an outcast, on whom respectable women look askance, and ignore as though you had never been!

Why did not you wait but one more day? One more day, and the sin need never have been, and you might have gone down to your grave a respected woman. Think no more of Bullion Castle; blot out from your mind that chamber which you hardly knew of your husband—go to your lover. That chamber should under any circumstances be far from your memory to-night—but as it is now! May you never hear of it; never picture it to yourself in the dark and sleepless watches of the night; never find it mixed in some mysterious way with every pleasure that you know, and doubly dyeing every sorrow that you feel.

For, stretched on that bed, stricken down

suddenly, lies Mr. Bullion, on the border-land
of life and death, a loud breathing audible
even outside the door, and bending over him
is Rosa, endeavouring all unconsciously by
her devotion now to atone for her mother's
vile sin.

What a treasure Rosa is at this time. All
her faculties rather sharpened than blunted
by the sudden twofold blow that has befallen
Bullion Castle. Telegraphing to Mr. Moorcraft; seeing the doctor, who has been
summoned hastily from Waterfield, and
behaving like a grown woman, rather than a
girl of seventeen.

And what of Richard Reef? He has got a
clue to the woman who used once to be Lady
Jane Bullion, and anxious for his master's
good name even now, is hurrying with all
speed to Dover to fetch her back before it be
too late.

It is so easy, he thinks, to hush it up. She
was called suddenly away. A friend was
sick, or a relative dying, and this great sin
need never be known. Alas! little did Reef

imagine that the last act of Mr. Bullion ere he was struck down by this fit of appoplexy would for ever prevent her sin being hushed up; for ever leave her an outcast upon the world.

The doctor from Waterfield gave no hope, and he was right. The breathing softens for a moment, and reason flickers over Mr. Bullion's face, and pressing Rosa's hand with almost a cheerful smile he falls back upon the pillow. Draw down the blinds of Bullion Castle to shut out the light of the rising summer sun; draw down the blinds and prepare to remove the crest of Bullion from the window panes. For the name of Bullion is extinct, and whilst that which once was Mr. Bullion lies rigid and cold in that gorgeous chamber, Lady Jane, in another room not quite so gorgeous, at the Lord Warden, turns in her sleep, with a smile upon her lips, and murmurs in her dreams the name of the man she loves.

CHAPTER IX.

THE sun is shining with unbroken splendour into one of the private sitting-rooms at the "Lord Warden;" shining on Lady Jane and her lover, as they sit at breakfast.

Lady Jane looks very lovely in her morning gown, lovely with all the matured beauty of fully developed womanhood, and Sir Harry Vale looks at her with a hardly-concealed smile upon his face, a smile of triumph.

A cool, calculating man, is Sir Harry, and I will not say that thoughts of a pecuniary nature had nothing to do with his elopement with Lady Jane.

The conversation is not particularly brilliant or flowing this morning, and is chiefly in connection with the crossing of the Channel, of which every woman who has ever been born, and many a man, too, by the way, is afraid.

Suddenly a knock at the door, and a waiter enters. An old man is waiting to see Lady Jane. Lady Jane is a courageous woman, but her face pales quickly at this announcement. An old man! Mr. Bullion might be described as an old man. Oh, what folly to stay the night at Dover; why did they not cross last night?

Sir Harry Vale looks uneasily around; he is no coward, but there is something of the aspect of a thief in his proceeding of yesterday that rises before him now in an unpleasant way, and he feels very like a man caught shooting pheasants on the wrong side of that agravating hedge we have looked over so often whilst the owner was away, that hedge which divides us from his choice preserves.

But on asking the waiter more particularly

it is at once evident that it is not Mr. Bullion who is waiting below, and Lady Jane thinks it wisest to see him in another room forthwith.

She goes thither, and in an instant is face to face with Richard Reef—Richard Reef, who with trouble and hurried travel looks ten years older than when she saw him last. And as she looks in his accusing, sorrowful face, in an instant, with overwhelming force, rises before her the sin she has committed, a sin which she now hears that need never have been committed had she waited but one more day.

"And yet, even yet," pleads old Reef, almost in tears, "nothing need be known. Mr. Bullion's name and yours need never bear a stain; no one guesses but that you have been called suddenly away; the note you left behind you Rosa burnt immediately. Only return, return at once, and mourn or try to mourn for all that has happened." Poor Reef grew almost eloquent in his distress.

For a moment Lady Jane hesitated, then she saw the wisdom of his words, for there was a vast estate, and like a woman she was quick enough to see that she might perhaps suffer, if she were found to have deserted her husband.

"Yes," she said slowly, after a minute's thought, "I will return to Bullion Castle."

And what of Sir Harry? Of course he was "extremely grieved," and "very much surprised," but saw at once the propriety of Lady Jane's instant return to Bullion Castle before, as he put it "anything had transpired," and when he was left alone whilst preparations were making for the return journey, could hardly help jumping for joy at his good fortune. Here was Lady Jane, one of the finest women in the county, a widow, completely in his power, and mistress of a fine estate and fifty thousand a year. Of course, within a year, he would marry her, and reside happily ever after at the Castle. A pleasant picture, truly.

What a journey back for Lady Jane!
What a journey, with every milestone bring-
ing her nearer to that death-chamber of the
man she had shamed, of the man who had
denied her nothing, and whom she had so
cruelly rewarded!

It was nearly dark when she arrived; she
had taken care that it should be so, and
almost as a thief in the night did she return
to the home over which she had formerly
reigned triumphant.

Trembling she walked across the hall,
feeling that each of those gorgeously-
liveried servants read her crime in her
face, and hated her beneath that deferential
manner.

Dreadful days those six to Lady Jane in
which the remains of Mr. Bullion were in the
house awaiting burial. Days in which the
undertaker reigned supreme, coming mysteriously every day and remaining closeted
with the dead, and retiring satisfied only
until the morrow.

Days with all the blinds down at the

Castle, and down at Rose Cottage, where poor little Rosa looked quite different but ten times more charming than ever in her first black dress.

Days in which Richard Reef wandered aimlessly about, feeling the weight of that awful secret bear him down. And Lady Jane could not bring herself to look upon the dead, but was obliged to listen to all the horrid details of that day from her maid.

How he had come home as well as usual, asked casually for herself, and on being informed she was from home had gone to the library. That presently the butler going in had found him busy with documents, and had indeed been asked to get a footman to witness Mr. Bullion's signature to one of the bulkiest of them. A document that Mr. Moorcraft had asked for and taken possession of on his being telegraphed for to the Castle.

And then how, later, he had been found senseless in a fit in his own room, where he

E

had half completed dressing for dinner. And
Lady Jane—Lady Jane the immovable—wept
as she had never wept in her life before; and
the domestics were surprised, and " had no
idea she was so fond of him."

CHAPTER X.

A DULL, lowering day, with the threatening roll of thunder in the distance. A day upon which the elements seemed angry and preparing vengeance.

An especially dull day at Bullion Castle. Numerous carriages, with their blinds closely drawn down, waiting in the stable-yard to offer the last tribute of their owners to the memory of the man whose hospitality they had so often received.

Lady Jane, dissolved in tears in her boudoir, and invisible, cannot, in the intervals of her grief, help thinking that the loss she has sustained will have many palliating features in the near future.

Several of the neighbours have been in-

E 2

vited to attend the funeral, for Mr. Bullion,
having no relatives, it is necessary that a
decent number of mourners should be in
attendance somehow.

All who were invited willingly attended,
for it is not every day in one's life that the
opportunity presents itself of hearing a
millionaire's will read.

The long procession winds slowly from the
gates of Bullion Castle, and not a little
surprise is evinced by the few who recognize
it to see James West's carriage amongst those
following—a handsome carriage, bearing upon
its panels the West arms, and their proud
motto, " *Non rogo, sed capio.*"

In the little village churchyard the cot-
tagers have assembled in great number,
for Mr. Bullion had been a homely, cha-
ritable man, and had endeared himself to
them all.

A slight pause at the church gates, and
then the solemn words we all know so well;
" We brought nothing into this world, and it
is certain we can carry nothing out. The

Lord gave, and the Lord taketh away; blessed be the name of the Lord."

In the church, draped with black, an occasional sob from women of the village makes the solemn hush all the more intense.

" And it is certain we can carry nothing out." The time of pains and triumphs alike is over ; we have acted our part of good or evil ; the play is over and the earth scattered, with a hollow sound, upon the coffin, marks the falling of the curtain, falling once and for all, never to rise again.

How small and insignificant it all seems to us now, with the silence only broken by that steady voice, which is repeating: "Forasmuch as it hath pleased Almighty God to take unto Himself our dear brother here departed." How small it all seems, this world and its trials and triumphs, as we look back upon it from the edge of that mysterious gulf, the grave ! And Mr. Moorcraft drops a wreath upon the coffin, and is heard to mutter softly to himself, " a million of money," and all is over.

That ghastly meal has been partaken of on the return from the church, and everyone who can decently do so has come into the library to hear the will read.

Mr. Moorcraft, with great solemnity, seated at the centre table, is deliberately wiping his spectacles, and gazing at the assembled company. Then he takes a bulky document from his breast pocket, unfolds it, and commences :—

" This is the last will and testament of John Bullion, of Bullion Castle, Blankshire, and Fenchurch-street, City, merchant, and is dated the 24th day of May, 188—."

A thrill goes through the company—it is the day he died !

There are several small legacies to old servants at the Castle and in London, and several bequests to charities, and then follows the body of the will, and Mr. Moorcraft reads with great unction ;—

" And the residue of my real and personal estate, together with my freehold property, known as Bullion Castle, my furniture, jewels, pictures, horses and carriages, and any balance which may be standing to my credit at my bankers, to—" Mr. Moorcraft pauses a moment, and looks at Lady Jane—"James West, Esquire, of Bramley Hall, in the county of Blankshire, as some small recompense for an injury which he once thought I did him."

And that was the end !

Then there is a sudden movement of the hearers towards Lady Jane, who has fallen senseless upon the floor.

There is a look of utter amazement upon every face, for Lady Jane's name has been omitted : in no way has she been noticed, as though she had never existed.

And she is borne to a bedroom of that mighty palace, in which she is now but a visitor on the sufferance of James West, a disgraced and ruined outcast.

The lights are shining again through the ruby-tinted shades in Lady Jane's boudoir, the night of the funeral, and the occupant is weeping bitterly, as she is collecting a few gowns and trifles together to take with her on

the morrow, when she leaves Bullion Castle
for ever; tears of mortification and disgrace.
She knows, none better, that by this time the
reason of that extraordinary will is known to
everyone, and a fear steals over her as she
wonders what its effect will be upon Sir
Harry Vale, the man she loves.

That she is a ruined woman she is well
aware, not only in a moral but also in a
worldly sense. . She had no money of her
own, and the only relative she has, a distant
one, will, she knows, repudiate that relationship the instant she hears the whole facts of
the case, and those facts can never be kept
secret. Sir Harry Vale is not rich, and she
is woman of the world enough to know that
liasons such as this do not last long—and
then, and then—and Lady Jane bursts again
into a flood of tears.

She feels to the full the bitterness of her
position—an outcast upon the world—and
thoughts of byegone times come back in full
force now, and with a twofold agony. She
thinks of a tiny, inoffensive being, once cast

off by her upon the world to shield herself from unpleasant consequences, cast off at an age which required all the tender nurture of a mother's care.

Ah, Lady Jane! you are not the first whose byegone sins have found them out. And she knew only too well that as far as James West was concerned, she was as though she had never existed.

And whilst Lady Jane is suffering all the tortures of remorse in the ruby-coloured boudoir at the Castle, Richard Reef and Rosa are standing by the newly-made grave in the quiet churchyard; Reef silently weeping for the master, whom he sees, as he looks back through that long vista of years—his life— had always been his best friend.

And Rosa is utterly confused and bewildered, and hardly realises that her lover is the richest man in Blankshire.

CHAPTER XI.

AFTER FIVE YEARS.

IT is a glorious summer morning at the Castle, with the birds singing merrily in every tree, and the lowing of cattle coming pleasantly from the distant fields.

James West and his wife, Rosa, are strolling about the rose garden, waiting for the coming round of the carriage that is to take them to the station, for they are going to London to-day for the season.

"I am almost sorry to leave the beautiful country," Rosa is saying, "just now, when it is at its best too; but we must go, if it is only to keep our promise to the Wright girls.

They are looking forward to their season with us." And James West, happier a thousand times than he ever expected to be, answers, "Yes, we must go, and there is that drawing-room to be got over; but, by the way, you are quite recovered I fancy from your alarms at that function. I suppose it is as in the old adage about familiarity, etc."

And then the carriage comes round, and Rosa runs off to bid a farewell to the sturdy heir of the Castle, aged three, who can talk quite intelligently already, and in whom Rosa fully believes she sees the future Prime Minister of England at the least.

*　　　*　　　*　　　*　　　*

And what of Lady Jane? She has been slowly sinking, step by step, into utter degradation. For Sir Harry Vale, on hearing of the fiasco of the will, prudently thought discretion the better part of valour, and having obtained his three months' leave, thought the best thing he could do was to utilise it in

endeavouring to woo fortune at Monte Carlo,
whither he went at once without communi-
cating with Lady Jane in any way, and
having there come across an elderly, amorous
lady of great wealth, fancied she would
answer his purpose better than the tables,
and so married her in a fortnight, and
mended the shattered fortunes of the house
of Vale.

Once only had Lady Jane seen West, and
that was three years after his marriage with
Rosa. Seen Rosa and him together, entering
the studio of a great artist, for James
West, " the millionaire,"—had become a
patron of art now. She had seen them both
for an instant, but it was sufficient to prove
to Lady Jane that the surmise she had often
made, when first she heard a rumour of
Rosa's doubtful parentage, was correct. In
the more fully developed womanhood of Rosa
she recognised the striking likeness to what
she had once been, and the doubt that
had been on her mind so long was removed; and as she staggered back to her

wretched lodgings she felt all the agonies
of that bitter curse—" what might have
been ! "

And Richard Reef is hale and hearty still,
and has long ago unburdened his mind of its
great secret to James West, and James West
knows more, on one subject at least, than he
tells his wife ; and when she talks, as she
does sometimes, of his generosity in marrying
the daughter of poor old humble Richard
Reef, he smiles a smile full of meaning as he
replies, " You are a lady though, Rosa, all
the same, and ten thousand times better than
the majority of them." And he gazes on the
strange likeness that calls up such memories
of the dead past, and knows that that horrible
tale about the frailty of the object of his
early love was only too true, and is thankful
that he has come off so well.

And we will leave him with his wife to
travel together till the end—until the end—
assured that it is only the one great King
who will sever them ; that their love will
burn steadily and true until that distant

day when there will again be a hush pervading the Castle, and for one of them the autumn of this life will be transformed suddenly, at one bound, into the eternal summer of the next.

THE END.

LONDON: PRINTED BY W. BURGESS, 56, SOUTHWARK STREET, S.E.